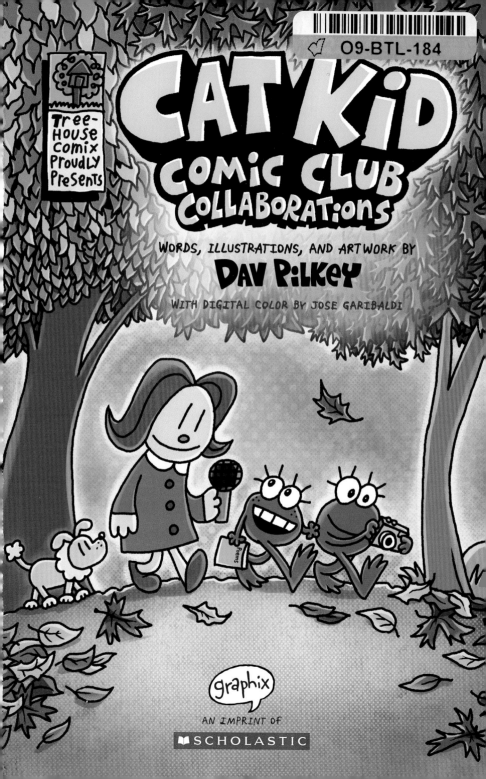

Tree-
HOUSE
Comix
Proudly
Presents

# CAT KID
## COMIC CLUB
### COLLABORATIONS

WORDS, ILLUSTRATIONS, AND ART WORK BY
**DAV PiLKEY**
WITH DIGITAL COLOR BY JOSE GARIBALDI

Poems

graphix

AN IMPRINT OF

**SCHOLASTIC**

Illustrations, 3-D models, photography,
and hand lettering by Dav Pilkey.

All mini comics colored by Dav Pilkey using pencils, markers,
pastels, ink, crayons, and colored pencils. 3-D models built out
of recycled cardboard, putty, wood, wire, plasticine, tape, glue,
broken toys, candy, graham crackers, frosting, gum, polyester
batting, styrofoam, and other repurposed items.

Digital Color by Jose Garibaldi | Flatting by Aaron Polk

Editor: Ken Geist | Editorial Team: Megan Peace and Jonah Newman
Book design by Dav Pilkey and Phil Falco
Creative Director: Phil Falco
Publisher: David Saylor

# CHAPTERS & COMICS

To Cece Bell, Tom Angleberger,
Oscar, and Charlie

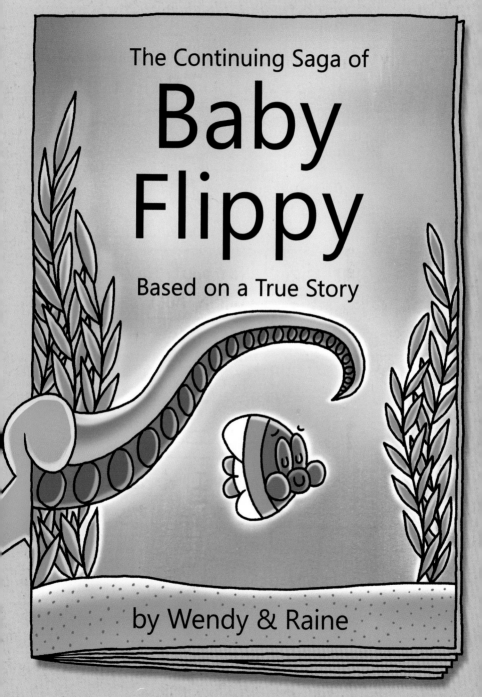

The Continuing Saga of

# Baby Flippy

Based on a True Story

by Wendy & Raine

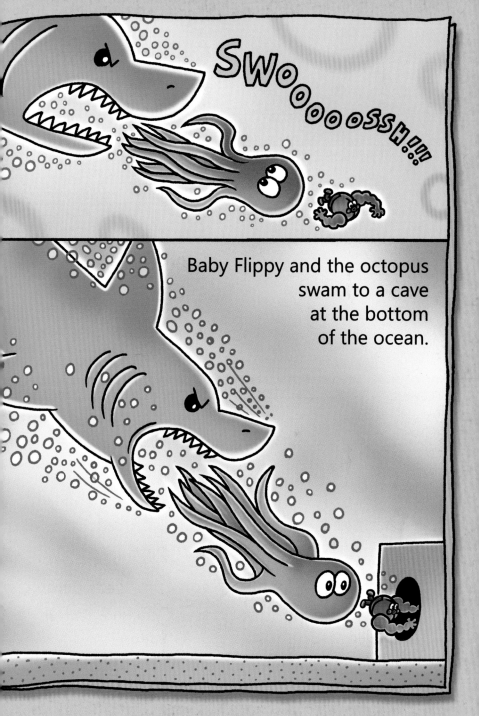

Baby Flippy and the octopus swam to a cave at the bottom of the ocean.

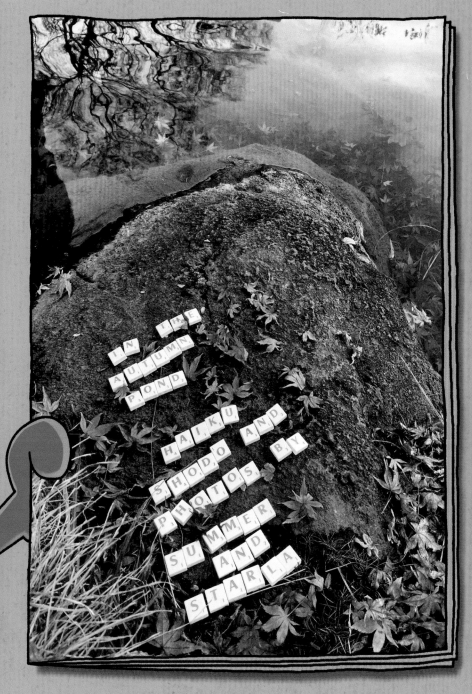

IN THE
AUTUMN,
POND

HAIKU    AND
SHODO    PHOTOS   BY
PHOTOS   BY
SUMMER
AND,
STARLA.

反
響
音

in the autumn pond
every leaf casts a shadow
each sound, an echo

見
性

the sun shows the way
but the sun is not the way
there's a difference

autumn days grow cold
yet in that winding downward
promises appear

休

乱舞

each star shines brightly
sparkling crisp on frigid twigs

dancing in breezes

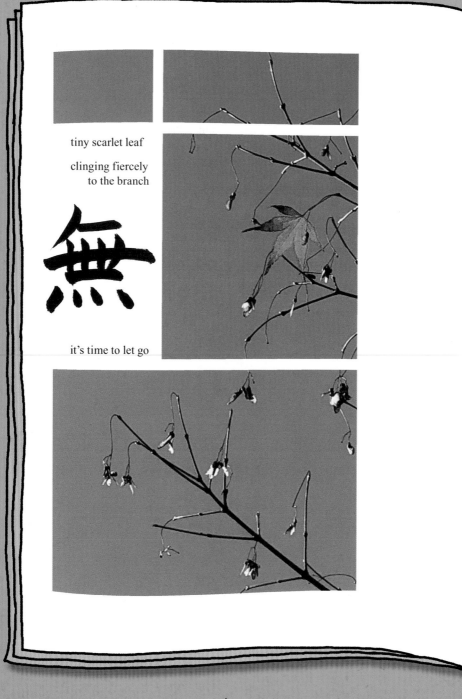

tiny scarlet leaf

clinging fiercely
to the branch

無

it's time to let go

little fallen leaves
your journey is not over

now you are a path

Each Shodo character can have many meanings.
These are some of the meanings for the ones we painted.

 = "han" – One meaning is "to return."

 = "kyou" – Sound or reverberate.
        Together, "hankyou" means "echo."

見 = "ken" – Seeing.

性 = "sho" – Nature, essense.
        Together, "kensho" means
        "to see one's nature from within."

休 = "yasumu" – To rest.

乱 = "ran" – Disorder.

舞 = "bu" – Dance.
        Together, "ranbu" means
        "boisterous dance."

無 = "mu" – Nothing. In this case,
        it means "although we may lose
        everything, new opportunities arise."

旅 = "tabi" – Journey.

Nao'omi Kuratani, Akemi Kobayashi, Shunsuke Okunishi,
*A New Dictionary of Kanji Usage* (Tokyo; Gakken Co., LTD., 1982).

Summer and Starla would like to
acknowledge and thank the artists who
continue to inspire them, including:

Shoko Kanazawa, who is one of Japan's
most highly respected Shodo artists. She
paints from her heart with giant brushes.
She also has Down's Syndrome.

And

Shozo Sato, author of *Shodo: The Quiet Art
of Japanese Zen Calligraphy* (Rutland:
Tuttle Publishing, 2014).

# CHAPTER 4

# Gilbert and Curly Heed the Call

CHUBBS McSPIDERBUTT
easy...
SPIDER

written and directed by
the hacker bros

Will the Not Very Nice Club EVER win?

Will our heroes EVER be violent enough to appear on kids' pajamas?

And WILL Scott EVER learn to read???

FIND OUT in the next epic Adventure of CHUBBS McSPIDERBUTT COMING SOON

140

143

# CHAPTER 8

# The Smallest Act of Kindness

157

161

162

165

174

175

215

# NOTES & FUN FACTS

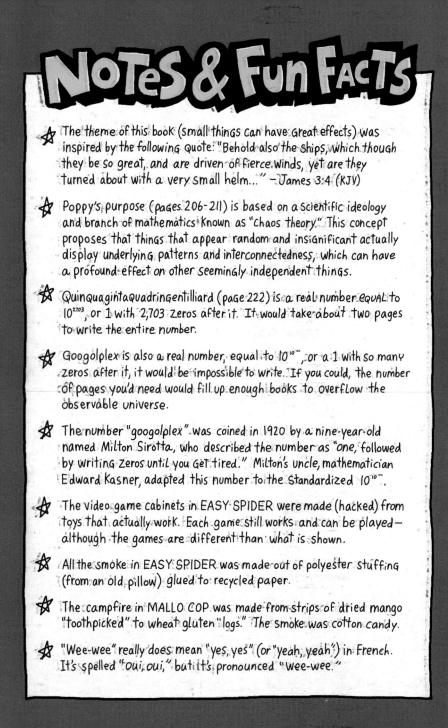

★ The theme of this book (small things can have Great effects) was inspired by the following quote: "Behold also the ships, which though they be so great, and are driven of fierce winds, yet are they turned about with a very small helm..." —James 3:4 (KJV)

★ Poppy's purpose (pages 206-211) is based on a scientific ideology and branch of mathematics known as "chaos theory." This concept proposes that things that appear random and insignificant actually display underlying patterns and interconnectedness, which can have a profound effect on other seemingly independent things.

★ Quinquagintaquadringentilliard (page 222) is a real number equal to $10^{2703}$, or 1 with 2,703 zeros after it. It would take about two pages to write the entire number.

★ Googolplex is also a real number, equal to $10^{10^{100}}$, or a 1 with so many zeros after it, it would be impossible to write. If you could, the number of pages you'd need would fill up enough books to overflow the observable universe.

★ The number "googolplex" was coined in 1920 by a nine-year-old named Milton Sirotta, who described the number as "one, followed by writing zeros until you get tired." Milton's uncle, mathematician Edward Kasner, adapted this number to the standardized $10^{10^{100}}$.

★ The video game cabinets in EASY SPIDER were made (hacked) from toys that actually work. Each game still works and can be played— although the games are different than what is shown.

★ All the smoke in EASY SPIDER was made out of polyester stuffing (from an old pillow) glued to recycled paper.

★ The campfire in MALLO COP was made from strips of dried mango "toothpicked" to wheat gluten "logs." The smoke was cotton candy.

★ "Wee-wee" really does mean "yes, yes" (or "yeah, yeah") in French. It's spelled "oui, oui," but it's pronounced "wee-wee."